My Mum

In memory of Our Doris, my fantastic mum
and for Jane, wonderful mother of our children.
A.B

MY MUM
A PICTURE CORGI BOOK 978 0 552 55234 9

First published in Great Britain by Doubleday,
an imprint of Random House Children's Books

Doubleday edition published 2005
Picture Corgi edition published 2006

9 10 8

Set in Goudy Old Style

Picture Corgi Books are published by Random House Children's Books,
61–63 Uxbridge Road, London W5 5SA,
a division of The Random House Group Ltd,
Addresses for companies within The Random House
Group Limited can be found at:www.randomhouse.co.uk/offices.htm

THE RANDOM HOUSE GROUP Limited Reg. No. 954009
www.kidsatrandomhouse.co.uk

A CIP catalogue record for this book is available from the British Library.

Printed in Singapore

My Mum
Anthony Browne

Picture Corgi

She's nice, my mum.

My mum's a fantastic cook,

and a brilliant juggler.

She's a great painter,

and the STRONGEST
woman in the world!

She's really nice, my mum.

My mum's a magic gardener.
She can make ANYTHING grow.

And she's a good fairy.
When I'm sad she can make me happy.

She can sing like an angel,

and roar like a lion.

She's really, REALLY nice, my mum.

My mum's as beautiful as a butterfly,

*and as comfy
as an
armchair.*

She's as soft as a kitten,

and as tough as a rhino.

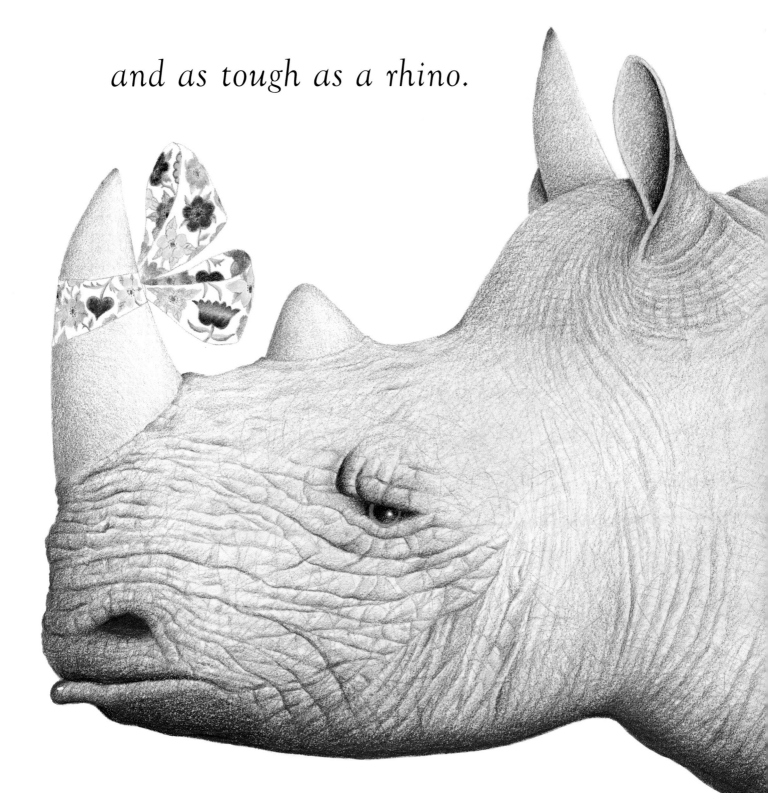

She's really, REALLY,
REALLY nice, my mum.

My mum could be a dancer,

or an astronaut.

She could be a film star,

THE BOSS

or the big boss. But she's MY mum.

She's a SUPERMUM!

And she makes me laugh. A lot.

I love my mum.

And you know what?

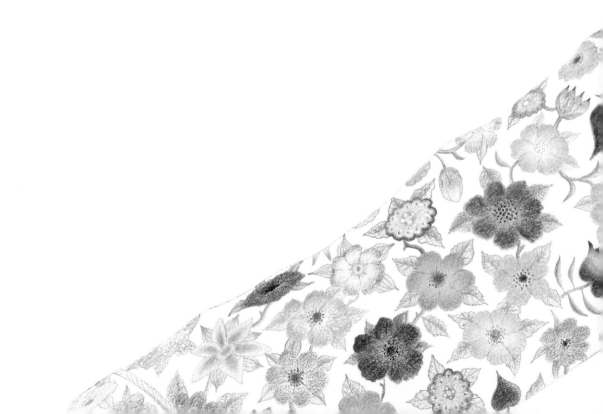

SHE LOVES ME!

(And she always will.)